A Thorny

Volume

Georg Ebers

(Translator: Clara Bell)

Alpha Editions

This edition published in 2023

ISBN : 9789357944540

Design and Setting By
Alpha Editions
www.alphaedis.com
Email - info@alphaedis.com

Contents

VOLUME 9.

CHAPTER XXVI

The lady Euryale's silent prayer was interrupted by the return of Alexander. He brought the clothes which Seleukus's wife had given him for Melissa. He was already dressed in his best, and crowned like all those who occupied the first seats in the Circus; but his festal garb accorded ill with the pained look on his features, from which every trace had vanished of the overflowing joy in life which had embellished them only this morning.

He had seen and heard things which made him feel that it would no longer be a sacrifice to give his life to save his sister.

Sad thoughts had flitted across his cheerful spirit like dark bats, even while he was talking with Melissa and her protectress, for he knew well how infinitely hard his father would find it to have to quit Alexandria; and if he himself fled with Melissa he would be obliged to give up the winning of fair Agatha. The girl's Christian father had indeed received him kindly, but had given him to understand plainly enough that he would never allow a professed heathen to sue for his daughter's hand. Besides this, he had met with other humiliations which placed themselves like a wall between him and his beloved, the only child of a rich and respected man. He had forfeited the right of appearing before Zeus as a suitor; for indeed he was no longer such as he had been only yesterday.

The news that Caracalla proposed to marry Melissa had been echoed by insolent tongues, with the addition that he, Alexander, had ingratiated himself with Caesar by serving him as a spy. No one had expressly said this to him; but, while he was hurrying through the city in Caesar's chariot, on the ladies' message, it had been made very plain to his apprehension. Honest men had avoided him—him to whom hitherto every one for whose regard he cared had held out a friendly hand; and much else that he had experienced in the course of this drive had been unpleasant enough to give rise to a change of his whole inner being.

The feeling that every one was pointing at him the finger of scorn, or of wrath, had never ceased to pursue him. And he had been under no illusion; for when he met the old sculptor Lysander, who only yesterday had so kindly told him and Melissa about Caesar's mother, as he nodded from the chariot his greeting was not returned; and the honest artist had waved his hand with a gesture which no Alexandrian could fail to understand as meaning, "I no longer know you, and do not wish to be recognized by you."

He had from his childhood loved Diodoros as a brother, and in one of the side streets, down which the chariot had turned to avoid the tumult in the Kanopic way, Alexander had seen his old friend. He had desired the charioteer to stop, and had leaped out on the road to speak to Diodoros and give him at once Melissa's message; but the young man had turned his back with evident displeasure, and to the painter's pathetic appeal, "But, at any rate, hear me!" he answered, sharply: "The less I hear of you and yours the better for me. Go on—go on, in Caesar's chariot!"

With this he had turned away and knocked at the door of an architect who was known to them both; and Alexander, tortured with painful feelings, had gone on, and for the first time the idea had taken possession of him that he had indeed descended to the part of spy when he had betrayed to Caesar what Alexandrian wit had to say about him. He could, of course, tell himself that he would rather have faced death or imprisonment than have betrayed to Caracalla the name of one of the gibers; still, he had to admit to himself that, but for the hope of saving his father and brother from death and imprisonment, he would hardly have done Caesar such service. The mercy shown to them was certainly too like payment, and his own part in the matter struck him as hateful and base. His fellow-townsmen had a right to bear him a grudge, and his friends to keep out of his way. A feeling came over him of bitter self-contempt, hitherto strange to him; and he understood for the first time how Philip could regard life as a burden and call it a malicious Danaus-gift of the gods. When, finally, in the Kanopic way, close in front of Seleukus's house, a youth unknown to him cried, scornfully, as the chariot was slowly making its way through the throng, "The brother-in-law of Tarautas!" he had great difficulty in restraining himself from leaping down and letting the rascal feel the weight of his fists. He knew, too, that Tarautas was the name of a hateful and bloodthirsty gladiator which had been given as a nickname to Caesar in Rome; and when he heard the insolent fellow's cry taken up by the mob, who shouted after him, "Tarautas's brother-in-law!" wherever he went, he felt as though he were being pelted with mire and stones.

It would have been a real comfort to him if the earth would have opened to swallow him with the chariot, to hide him from the sight of men. He could have burst out crying like a child that has been beaten. When at last he was safe inside Seleukus's house, he was easier; for here he was known; here he would be understood. Berenike must know what he thought of Caesar's suit, and seeing her wholesome and honest hatred, he had sworn to himself that he would snatch his sister from the hands of the tyrant, if it were to lead him to the most agonizing death.

While she was engaged in selecting a dress for her protegee, he related to the lady Euryale what had happened to him in the street and in the house of Seleukus. He had been conducted past the soldiers in the vestibule and impluvium to the lady's private rooms, and there he had been witness to a violent matrimonial dispute. Seleukus had previously delivered to his wife

Caesar's command that she should appear in the Amphitheater with the other noble dames of the city. Her answer was a bitter laugh, and a declaration that she would mingle with the spectators in none but mourning robes. Thereupon her husband, pointing out to her the danger to which such conduct would expose them, had raised objections, and she at last had seemed to yield. When Alexander joined her he had found her in a splendid dress of shining purple brocade, her black hair crowned with a wreath of roses, and a splendid diadem; a garland of roses hung across her bosom, and precious stones sparkled round her throat and arms. In short, she was arrayed like a happy mother for her daughter's wedding-day.

Soon after Alexander's arrival Seleukus had come in, and this conspicuously handsome dress, so unbecoming to the matron's age, and so unlike her usual attire-chosen, evidently, to put the monstrosity of Caesar's demand in the strongest light—had roused her husband's wrath. He had expressed his dissatisfaction in strong terms, and again pointed out to her the danger in which such a daring demonstration might involve them; but this time there was no moving the lady; she would not despoil herself of a single rose. After she had solemnly declared that she would appear in the Circus either as she thought fit or not at all, her husband had left her in anger.

"What a fool she is!" Euryale exclaimed.

Then she showed him a white robe of beautiful bombyx, woven in the isle of Kos, which she had decided on for Melissa, and a peplos with a border of tender sea-green; and Alexander approved of the choice.

Time pressed, and Euryale went at once to Melissa with the new festal raiment. Once more she nodded kindly to the girl, and begged her, as she herself had something to discuss with Alexander, to allow the waiting-woman to dress her. She felt as if she were bringing the robe to a condemned creature, in which she was to be led to execution, and Melissa felt the same.

Euryale then returned to the painter, and bade him end his narrative.

The lady Berenike had forthwith desired Johanna to pack together all the dead Korinna's festal dresses. Alexander had then followed her guidance, accompanying her to a court in the slaves' quarters, where a number of men were awaiting her. These were the captains of Seleukus's ships, which were now in port, and the superintendents of his granaries and offices, altogether above a hundred freedmen in the merchant's service. Each one seemed to know what he was here for.

The matron responded to their hearty greetings with a word of thanks, and added, bitterly:

"You see before you a mourning mother whom a ruthless tyrant compels to go to a festival thus—thus—only look at me—bedizened like a peacock!"

At this the bearded assembly gave loud expression to their dissatisfaction, but Berenike went on "Melapompus has taken care to secure good places; but he has wisely not taken them all together. You are all free men; I have no orders to give you. But, if you are indeed indignant at the scorn and heartache inflicted on your lord's wife, make it known in the Circus to him who has brought them on her. You are all past your first youth, and will carefully avoid any rashness which may involve you in ruin. May the avenging gods aid and protect you!"

With this she had turned her back on the multitude; but Johannes, the Christian lawyer, the chief freedman of the household, had hurried into the court-yard, just in time to entreat her to give up this ill-starred demonstration, and to extinguish the fire she had tried to kindle. So long as Caesar wore the purple, rebellion against him, to whom the Divinity had intrusted the sovereignty, was a sin. The scheme she was plotting was meant to punish him who had pained her; but she forgot that it might cost these brave men, husbands and fathers, their life or liberty. The vengeance she called on them to take might be balm to the wounds of her own heart; but if Caesar in his wrath brought destruction down on these, her innocent instruments, that balm would turn to burning poison.

These words, whispered to her with entire conviction, had not been without their effect. For some minutes Berenike had stared gloomily at the ground; but then she had again approached the assembly, to repeat the warning given her by the Christian, whom all respected, and by whom some indeed had been persuaded to be baptized.

"Johannes is right," she ended. "This ill-used heart did wrong when it sent up its cry of anguish before you. Rather will I be trodden under foot by the enemy, as is the manner of the Christians, than bring such misfortune on innocent men, who are so faithful to our house. Be cautious, then. Give no overt expression to your feelings. Let each one who feels too weak to control his wrath, avoid the Circus; and those who go, keep still if they feel moved to act in my behalf. One thing only you may do. Tell every one, far and wide, what I had purposed. What others may do, they themselves must answer for."

The Christian had strongly disapproved of this last clause; but Berenike had paid no heed, and had left the court-yard, followed by Alexander.

The shouts of the indignant multitude had rung in their ears, and, in spite of her warning, they had sounded like a terrible threat. Johannes, to be sure, had remained, to move them to moderation by further remonstrances.

"What were the mad creatures plotting?" Euryale anxiously broke in; and he hastily went on "They call Caesar by no name but Tarautas; every mouth is full of gibes and rage at the new and monstrous taxes, the billeting of the troops, and the intolerable insolence of the soldiery, which Caracalla wickedly encourages. His contemptuous indifference has deeply offended the heads of the town. And then his suit to my sister! Young and old are wagging their tongues over it."

"It would be more like them to triumph in it," said the matron, interrupting him. "An Alexandrian in the purple, on the throne of the Caesars!"

"I too had hoped that," cried Alexander, "and it seemed so likely. But who can understand the populace? Every woman in the place, I should have thought, would hold her head higher, at the thought that an Alexandrian girl was empress; but it was from the women that I heard the most vindictive and shameless abuse. I heard more than enough; for, as we got closer to the Serapeum, the more slowly was the chariot obliged to proceed, to make its way through the crowd. And the things I heard! I clinch my fists now as I only think of them.—And what will it be in the Circus? What will not Melissa have to endure!"

"It is envy," the matron murmured to herself; but she was immediately silent, for the young girl came toward them, out of the bedroom. Her toilet was complete; the beautiful white dress became her well. The wreath of roses, with diamond dewdrops, lay lightly on her hair, the snake-shaped bracelet which her imperial suitor had sent her clasped her white arm, and her small head, somewhat bent, her pale, sweet face, and large, bashful, inquiring, drooping eyes formed such an engaging, modest, and unspeakably touching picture, that Euryale dared to hope that even in the Circus none but hardened hearts could harbor a hostile feeling against this gentle, pure blossom, slightly drooping with silent sorrow. She could not resist the impulse to kiss Melissa, and the half-formed purpose ripened within her to venture the utmost for the child's protection. The pity in her heart had turned to love; and when she saw that to this sweet creature, at the mere sight of whom her heart went forth, the most splendid jewels, in which any other girl would have been glad to deck herself, were as a heavy burden to be borne but sadly, she felt it a sacred duty to comfort her and lighten this trial, and shelter Melissa, so far as was in her power, from insult and humiliation.

It was many years since she had visited the Amphitheater, where the horrible butchery was an abomination to her; but to-day her heart bade her conquer her old aversion, and accompany the girl to the Circus.

Had not Melissa taken the place in her heart of her lost daughter? Was not she, Euryale, the only person who, by showing herself with Melissa and declaring herself her friend, could give the people assurance that the girl, who was exposed to misapprehension and odium by the favor she had met with from the ruthless and hated sovereign, was in truth pure and lovable? Under her guardianship, by her side, the girl, as she knew, would be protected from misapprehension and insult; and she, an old woman and a Christian, should she evade the first opportunity of taking up a cross in imitation of the Divine Master, among whose followers she joyfully counted herself—though secretly, for fear of men? All this flashed through her mind with the swiftness of lightning, and her call, "Doris!" addressed to her waiting-woman, was so clear and unexpected that Melissa's overstrung nerves were startled. She looked up at the lady in amazement, as, without a word of explanation, she said to the woman who had hurried in:

"The blue robe I wore at the festival of Adonis, my mother's diadem, and a large gem with the head of Serapis for my shoulder. My hair—oh, a veil will cover it! What does it matter for an old woman?—You, child, why do you look at me in such amazement? What mother would allow a pretty young daughter to appear alone in the Circus? Besides, I may surely hope that it will confirm your courage to feel that I am at your side. Perhaps the populace may be moved a little in your favor if the wife of the high-priest of their greatest god is your companion."

But she could scarcely end her speech, for Melissa had flown into her arms, exclaiming, "And you will do this for me?" while Alexander, deeply touched by gratitude and joy, kissed her thin arm and the hem of her peplos.

While Melissa helped the matron to change her dress—in the next room Alexander paced to and fro in great unrest. He knew the Alexandrians, and there was not the slightest doubt but that the presence of this universally revered lady would make them look with kindlier eyes on his sister. Nothing else could so effectually impress them with the entire propriety of her appearance in the Circus. The more seriously he had feared that Melissa might be deeply insulted and offended by the rough demonstrations of the mob, the more gratefully did his heart beat; nay, his facile nature saw in this kind act the first smile of returning good fortune.

He only longed to be hopeful once more, to enjoy the present—as so many philosophers and poets advised—and especially the show in the Circus, his last pleasure, perhaps; to forget the imminent future.

The old bright look came back to his face; but it soon vanished, for even while he pictured himself in the amphitheatre, he remembered that there, too, his former acquaintances might refuse to speak to him; that the odious names of "Tarautas' brother-in-law" or of "traitor" might be shouted after him on the road. A cold chill came over him, and the image of pretty Ino rose up before him—Ino, who had trusted in his love; and to whom, of all others, he had given cause to accuse him of false- heartedness. An unpleasant sense came over him of dissatisfaction with himself, such as he, who always regarded self-accusation, repentance, and atonement as a foolish waste of life, had never before experienced.

The fine, sunny autumn day had turned to a sultry, dull evening, and Alexander went to the window to let the sea-breeze fan his dewy brow; but he soon heard voices behind him, for Euryale and Melissa had re-entered the room, followed by the house-steward, who presented to his mistress a sealed tablet which a slave had just brought from Philostratus. The women had been talking of Melissa's vow; and Euryale had promised her that, if Fate should decide against Caesar, she would convey the girl to a place of safety, where she could certainly not be discovered, and might look forward in peace to the future. Then she had impressed on her that, if things should be otherwise ordered, she must endure even the unendurable with patience, as an obedient wife, as empress, but still ever conscious of the solemn and beneficent power she might wield in her new position.

The tablets would now settle the question; and side by side the two women hastily read the missive which Philostratus had written on the wax, in his fine, legible hand. It was as follows:

"The condemned have ceased to live. Your efforts had no effect but to hasten their end. Caesar's desire was to rid you of adversaries even against your will. Vindex and his nephew are no more; but I embarked soon enough to escape the rage of him who might have attained the highest favors of fortune if he had but known how to be merciful."

"God be praised!—but alas, poor Vindex!" cried Euryale, as she laid down the tablets. But Melissa kissed her, and then exclaimed to her brother:

"Now all doubts are at an end. I may fly. He himself has settled the matter!"

Then she added, more gently, but still urgently "Do you take care of my father, and Philip, and of yourself. The lady Euryale will protect me. Oh, how thankful am I!"

She looked up to heaven with fervent devotion Euryale whispered to them: "My plan is laid. As soon as the performance is over, Alexander shall take you home, child, to your father's house; you must go in one of Caesar's chariots. Afterward come back here with your brother; I will wait for you below. But now we will go together to the Circus, and can discuss the details on our way. You, my young friend, go now and order away the imperial litter; bid my steward to have the horses put to my covered harmamaxa. There is room in it for us all three."

By the time Alexander returned, the daylight was waning, and the clatter of the chariots began to be audible which conveyed Caesar's court to the Circus.

CHAPTER XXVIL

The great Amphitheatre of Dionysus was in the Bruchium, the splendid palatial quarter of the city, close to the large harbor between the Choma and the peninsula of Lochias. Hard by the spacious and lofty rotunda, in which ten thousand spectators could be seated, stood the most fashionable gymnasia and riding-schools. These buildings, which had been founded long since by the Ptolemaic kings, and had been repeatedly extended and beautified, formed, with the adjoining schools for gladiators and beast-fighters, and the stables for wild beasts from every part of the world, a little town by themselves.

At this moment the amphitheatre looked like a beehive, of which every cell seems to be full, but in which a whole swarm expects yet to find room. The upper places, mere standing-room for the common people, and the cheaper seats, had been full early in the day. By the afternoon the better class of citizens had come in, if their places were not reserved; and now, at sunset, those who were arriving in litters and chariots, just before the beginning of the show, were for the most part in Caesar's train, court officials, senators, or the rich magnates of the city.

The strains of music were by this time mingling with the shouting and loud talk of the spectators, or of the thousands who were crowding round the building without hoping to obtain admission. But even for them there was plenty to be seen. How delightful to watch the well-dressed women, and the men of rank and wealth, crowned with wreaths, as they dismounted; to see the learned men and artists arrive—more or less eagerly applauded, according to the esteem in which they were held by the populace! The most splendid sight of all was the procession of priests, with Timotheus, the high-priest of Serapis, at their head, and by his side the priest of Alexander, both marching with dignity under a canopy. They were followed by the animals to be slaughtered for sacrifice, and the images of the gods and the deified Caesars, which were to be placed in the arena, as the most worshipful of all the spectators. Timotheus wore the splendid insignia of his office; the priest of Alexander was in purple, as being the idiologos and head of all the temples of Egypt, and representative of Caesar.

The advent of the images of the Caesars gave rise to a sort of judgment of the dead: for the mob hailed that of Julius Caesar with enthusiasm, that of Augustus, with murmurs of disapproval; when Caligula appeared, he was hissed; while the statues of Vespasian, Titus, Hadrian, and Antonine, met with loud acclamations. That of Septimius Severus, Caracalla's father, to whom the town owed many benefits, was very well received. The images of the gods, too, had very various fates. Serapis, and Alexander, the divine hero of the town, were enthusiastically welcomed, while scarcely a voice was heard on the approach of Zeus-Jupiter and Ares-Mars. They were regarded as the gods of the hated Romans.

The companies of the imperial body-guard, who were placed about the amphitheatre, found no great difference, so long as it was daylight, between the crowd round the Circus of Alexandria and that by the Tiber. What chiefly struck them was the larger number of dusky faces, and the fanciful garb of the Magians. The almost naked rabble, too, with nothing on but a loin-cloth, who wriggled in and out of the throng, ready for any service or errand, formed a feature unknown at Rome. But, as it grew darker, the Romans began to perceive that it was not for nothing that they had come hither.

At Rome, when some great show was promised, of beast-fighting, gladiators, and the like, there were, no doubt, barbarian princes to be seen, and envoys from the remotest ends of the earth in strange and gorgeous array; and there, too, small wares of every kind were for sale. By the Tiber, again, night shows were given, with grand illuminations, especially for the feast of Flora; but here, as soon as the sun had set, and the sports were about to begin, the scene was one never to be forgotten. Some of the ladies who descended from the litters, wore garments of indescribable splendor; the men even displayed strange and handsome costumes as they were helped out of their gilt and plated chariots by their servants. What untold wealth must these men have at their command, to be able to dress their slaves in gold and silver brocade; and the runners, who kept up with the swiftest horses, must have lungs of iron! The praetorians, who had not for many a day seen anything to cause them to forget the motto of the greatest philosopher among their poets— never to be astonished at anything—repeatedly pushed each other with surprise and admiration; nay, the centurion Julius Martialis, who had just now had a visit in camp from his wife and children, in defiance of orders, while Caesar himself was looking on, struck his fist on his greaves, and, exclaiming loudly, "Look out!" pointed to Seleukus's chariot, for which four runners, in tunics with long sleeves, made of sea-green bombyx, richly embroidered with silver, were making a way through the crowd.

The barefooted lads, with their nimble, gazellelike legs, were all well looking, and might have been cast all in one mold. But what struck the centurion and his comrades as most remarkable in their appearance were the flash and sparkle from their slender ankles, as the setting sun suddenly shot a fleeting ray through a rift in the heavy clouds. Each of these fellows wore on his legs gold bands set with precious stones, and the rubies which glittered on the harness of Seleukus's horse were of far greater value.

He, as master of the festival, had come betimes, and this was the first of many such displays of wealth which followed each other in quick succession, as soon as the brief twilight of Egypt had given way to darkness, and the lighting up of the Circus was begun.

Here came a beautifully dressed woman in a roomy litter, over which waved a canopy entirely of white ostrich-plumes, which the evening breeze swayed like a thicket of fern-leaves. This throne was borne by ten black and ten white slave-girls, and before it two fair children rode on tame ostriches. The tall heir of a noble house, who, like Caesar at Rome, belonged to the "Blues," drove his own team of four splendid white horses; and he himself was covered with turquoises, while the harness was set with cut sapphires.

The centurion shook his head in silent admiration. His face had been tanned in many wars, both in the East and West, and he had fought even in distant Caledonia, but the low forehead, loose under lip, and dull eye spoke of small gifts of intellect. Nevertheless, he was not lacking in strength of will, and was regarded by his comrades as a good beast of burden who would submit to a great deal before it became too much for him. But then he would break out like a mad bull, and he might long ago have risen to higher rank, had he not once in such a fit of passion nearly throttled a fellow-soldier. For this crime he had been severely punished, and condemned to begin again at the bottom of the ladder. He owed it chiefly to the young tribune Aurelius Apollinaris that he had very soon regained the centurion's staff, in spite of his humble birth; he had saved that officer's life in the war with the Armenians—to be here, in Alexandria, cruelly mutilated by the hand of his sovereign.

The centurion had a faithful heart. He was as much attached to the two noble brothers as to his wife and children, for indeed he owed them much; and if the service had allowed it he would long since have made his way to the house of Seleukus to learn how the wounded tribune was faring. But he had not time even to see his own family, for his younger and richer comrades, who wanted to enjoy the pleasures of the city, had put upon him no small share of their own duties. Only this morning a young soldier of high birth, who had begun his career at the same time as Martialis, had promised him some tickets of admission to the evening's performance in the Circus if he would take his duty on guard outside the amphitheatre. And this offer had been very welcome to the centurion, for he thus found it possible to give those he loved best, his wife and his mother, the greatest treat which could be offered to any Alexandrian. And now, when anything noteworthy was to be seen outside, he only regretted that he had already some time since conducted them to their seats in one of the upper rows. He would have liked that they, too, should have seen the horses and the chariots and the "Blue" charioteer's turquoises and sapphires; although a decurion observed, as he saw them, that a Roman patrician would scorn to dress out his person with such barbaric splendor, and an Alexandrian of the praetorian guard declared that his fellow-citizens of Greek extraction thought more of a graceful fold than of whole strings of precious stones.

"But why, then, was this 'Blue' so vehemently hailed by the mob!" asked a Pannonian in the guard.

"The mob!" retorted the Alexandrian, scornfully. "Only the Syrians and other Asiatics. Look at the Greeks. The great merchant Seleukus is the richest of them all, but splendid as his horses, his chariots, and his slaves are, he himself wears only the simple Macedonian mantle. Though it is of costly material, who would suspect it? If you see a man swaggering in such a blaze of gems you may wager your house—if you have one—that his birthplace lies not very far from Syria."

"Now, that one, in a mother-of-pearl shell on two wheels, is the Jew Poseidonius," the Pannonian put in. "I am quartered on his father. But he is dressed like a Greek."

At this the centurion, in his delight at knowing something, opened his mouth with a broad grin: "I am a native here," said he, "and I can tell you the Jew would make you answer for it if you took him for anything but a Greek."

"And quite right," added another soldier, from Antioch. "The Jews here are many, but they have little in common with those in Palestine. They wish to pass for Greeks; they speak Greek, assume Greek names, and even cease to believe in the great God their father; they study Greek philosophy, and I know one who worships in the Temple of Serapis."

"Many do the same in Rome," said a man of Ostia. "I know an epigram which ridicules them for it."

At this point they were interrupted, for Martialis pointed to a tall man who was coming toward them, and whom his sharp eye had recognized as Macrinus, the prefect of the praetorians. In an instant the soldiers were erect and rigid, but still many a helmeted head was turned toward the spot where their chief stood talking in an undertone to the Magian Serapion.

Macrinus had persuaded Caesar to send for the exorciser, to test his arts. Immediately after the performance, however late it might be, the Magian was to be admitted to his presence.

Serapion thanked the prefect, and then whispered to him, "I have had a second revelation."

"Not here!" exclaimed Macrinus, uneasily, and, leading away his handsome little son, he turned toward the entrance.

Dusk, meanwhile, had given way to darkness, and several slaves stood ready to light the innumerable little lamps which were to illuminate the outside of the Circus. They edged the high arches which surrounded the two lower stories, and supported the upper ranks of the enormous circular structure. Separated only by narrow intervals, the rows of lights formed a glittering series of frames which outlined the noble building and rendered it visible from afar.

The arches on the ground-floor led to the cells from which the men and beasts were let out into the arena; but some, too, were fitted with shops, where flowers and wreaths, refreshments, drinks, handkerchiefs, fans, and other articles in request, were sold. On the footway between the building and the row of pitch torches which surrounded it, men and women in thousands were walking to and fro. Smart, inquisitive girls were pushing their way singly or in groups, and their laughter drowned the deep, tragical voices of the soothsayers and Magians who announced their magic powers to the passersby. Some of these even made their way into the waiting-rooms of the gladiators and wrestlers, who to-day so greatly needed their support that, in spite of severe and newly enforced prohibitions, many a one stole out into the crowd to buy some effectual charm or protecting amulet.

Where the illuminations were completed, attempts of another kind were being made to work upon the mood of the people; nimble-tongued fellows— some in the service of Macrinus and some in that of the anxious senate— were distributing handkerchiefs to wave on Caesar's approach, or flowers to strew in his path. More than one, who was known for a malcontent, found a gold coin in his hand, with the image of the monarch he was expected to hail; and on the way by which Caesar was to come many of those who awaited him wore the caracalla. These were for the most part bribed, and their acclamations were to mollify the tyrant's mood.

As soon as the prefect had disappeared within the building, the praetorian ranks fell out again. It was lucky that among them were several Alexandrians, besides the centurion Martialis, who had not long been absent from their native town; for without them much would have remained incomprehensible. The strangest thing to foreign eyes was a stately though undecorated harmamaxa, out of which stepped first a handsome wreathed youth, then a matron of middle age, and at last an elegantly dressed girl, whose rare beauty made even Martialis—who rarely noticed women— exclaim, "Now, she is to my taste the sweetest-thing of all."

But there must have been something very remarkable about these three; for when they appeared the crowd broke out at first in loud shouts and outcries, which soon turned to acclamations and welcome, though through it all shrill whistles and hisses were heard.

"Caesar's new mistress, the daughter of a gemcutter!" the Alexandrian muttered to his comrades. That handsome boy is her brother, no doubt. He is said to be a mean sycophant, a spy paid by Caesar."

"He?" said an older centurion, shaking his scarred head. "Sooner would I believe that the shouts of the populace were intended for the old woman and not for the young one."

"Then a sycophant he is and will remain," said the Alexandrian with a laugh. "For, as a matter of fact, it is the elder lady they are greeting, and, by Heracles, she deserves it! She is the wife of the high-priest of Serapis. There are few poor in this city to whom she has not done a kindness. She is well able, no doubt, for her husband is the brother of Seleukus, and her father, too, sat over his ears in gold."

"Yes, she is able," interrupted Martialis, with a tone of pride, as though it were some credit to himself. "But how many have even more, and keep their purse-strings tight! I have known her since she was a child, and she is the best of all that is good. What does not the town owe to her! She risked her life to move Caesar's father to mercy toward the citizens, after they had openly declared against him and in favor of his rival Pescennius Niger. And she succeeded, too."

"Why, then, are they whistling?" asked the older centurion.

"Because her companion is a spy," repeated the Alexandrian. "And the girl— In Caesar's favor! But, after all, which of you all would not gladly see his sister or his niece Caesar's light of love?"

"Not I!" cried Martialis. "But the man who speaks ill of that girl only does so because he likes blue eyes best. The maiden who comes in the lady Euryale's chariot is spotless, you may swear."

"Nay, nay," said the younger Alexandrian soothingly. "That black-haired fellow and his companions would whistle another tune if they knew any evil of her, and she would not be in the lady Euryale's company—that is the chief point—. But, look there! The shameless dogs are stopping their way! 'Green' to a man.—But here come the lictors."

"Attention!" shouted Martialis, firmly resolved to uphold the guardians of the peace, and not to suffer any harm to the matron and her fair companion; for Euryale's husband was the brother of Seleukus, whom his father and father-in-law had served years ago, while in the villa at Kanopus his mother and wife were left in charge to keep it in order. He felt that he was bound in duty to the merchant, and that all who were of that household had a right to count on his protection. But no active measures were needed; a number of "Blues" had driven off the "Greens" who had tried to bar Alexander's way, and the lictors came to their assistance.

A young man in festal array, who had pushed into the front rank of the bystanders, had looked on with panting breath. He was very pale, and the thick wreath he wore was scarcely sufficient to hide the bandage under it. This was Diodoros, Melissa's lover. After resting awhile at his friend's house he had been carried in a litter to the amphitheatre, for he could yet hardly walk. His father being one of the senators of the town, his family had a row of seats in the lowest and best tier; but this, on this occasion, was entirely given up to Caesar and his court. Consequently the different members of the senate could have only half the usual number of seats. Still, the son of Polybius might in any case claim two in his father's name; and his friend Timon—who had also provided him with suitable clothing—had gone to procure the tickets from the curia. They were to meet at the entrance leading to their places, and it would be some little time yet before Timon could return.

Diodoros had thought he would behold his imperial rival; however, instead of Caracalla he had seen the contemptuous reception which awaited Alexander and Melissa, from some at least of the populace. Still, how fair and desirable had she seemed in his eyes, whom, only that morning, he had been blessed in calling his! As he now moved away from the main entrance, he asked himself why it was such torture to him to witness the humiliation of a being who had done him such a wrong, and whom he thought he hated and scorned so utterly. Hardly an hour since he had declared to Timon that he had rooted his love for Melissa out of his heart. He himself would feel the better for using the whistle he wore, in derision of her, and for seeing her faithlessness punished by the crowd. But now? When the insolent uproar went up from the "Greens," whose color he himself wore, he had found it difficult to refrain from rushing on the cowardly crew and knocking some of them down.

He now made his way with feeble steps to the entrance where he was to meet his friend. The blood throbbed in his temples, his mouth was parched, and, as a fruit-seller cried her wares from one of the archways, he took a few apples from her basket to refresh himself with their juice. His hand trembled, and the experienced old woman, observing the bandage under his wreath, supposed him to be one of the excited malcontents who had perhaps already fallen into the hands of the lictors. So, with a significant grin, she pointed under the table on which her fruit-baskets stood, and said "I have plenty of rotten ones. Six in a wrapper, quite easy to hide under your cloak. For whom you will. Caesar has given the golden apple of Paris to a goddess of this town. I should best like to see these flung at her brother, the sycophant."

"Do you know them?" asked Diodoros, hoarsely.

"No," replied the old woman. "No need for that. I have plenty of customers and good ears. The slut broke her word with a handsome youth of the town for the sake of the Roman, and they who do such things are repaid by the avenging gods." Diodoros felt his knees failing under him, and a wrathful answer was on his lips, when the huckster suddenly shouted like mad: "Caesar, Caesar! He is coming."

The shouts of the crowd hailing their emperor had already become audible through the heavy evening air, at first low and distant, and louder by degrees. They now suddenly rose to a deafening uproar, and while the sound rolled on like approaching thunder, broken by shrill whistles suggesting lightning, the sturdy old apple-seller clambered unaided on to her table, and shouted with all her might:

"Caesar! Here he is!—Hail, hail, hail to great Caesar!"

At the imminent risk of tumbling off her platform, she bent low down to reach under the table for the blue cloth which covered her store of rotten apples, snatched it off, and waved it with frantic enthusiasm, as though her elderly heart had suddenly gone forth to the very man for whom a moment ago she had been ready to sell her disgusting missiles. And still she shouted in ringing tones, "Hail, hail, Caesar!" again and again, with all her might, till there was no breath left in her overbuxom, panting breast, and her round face was purple with the effort. Nay, her emotion was so vehement that the bright tears streamed down her fat cheeks.

And every one near was shrieking like the applewoman, "Hail, Caesar!" and it was only where the crowd was densest that a sharp whistle now and then rent the roar of acclamations.

Diodoros, meanwhile, had turned to look at the main entrance, and, carried away by the universal desire to see, had perched himself on an unopened case of dried figs. His tall figure now towered far above the throng, and he set his teeth as he heard the old woman, almost speechless with delight, gasp out:

"Lovely! wonderful! He would never have found the like in Rome. Here, among us—"

But the cheers of the multitude now drowned every other sound. Fathers or mothers who had children with them lifted them up as high as they could; where a small man stood behind a tall one, way was willingly made, for it would have been a shame to hinder his view of such a spectacle. Many had already seen the great monarch in his shining, golden chariot, drawn by four splendid horses; but such an array of torch-bearers as now preceded Caracalla was a thing never seen within the memory of the oldest or most traveled man.

Three elephants marched before him and three came behind, and all six carried in their trunks blazing torches, which they held now low and now aloft to light his road. To think that beasts could be trained to such a service! And that here, in Alexandria, such a display could be made before the haughty and pampered Romans!

The chariot stood still, and the black Ethiopians who guided the huge four-footed torch-bearers took the three leaders to join their fellows behind the chariot. This really was a fine sight; this could not but fill the heart of every one who loved his native town with pride and delight. For what should a man ever shout himself hoarse, if not for such a splendid and unique show? Diodoros himself could not take his eyes off the elephants. At first he was delighted with them, but presently the sight annoyed him even more than it had pleased him; for he reflected that the tyrant, the villain, his deadly enemy, would certainly take to himself the applause bestowed on the clever beasts. With this, he grasped the reed pipe in the breast of his tunic. He had been on the point of using it before now, to retaliate on Melissa for some portion of the pain she had inflicted on him. At this thought, however, the paltriness of such revenge struck him with horror, and with a hasty impulse he snapped the pipe in two, and flung the pieces on the ground in front of the apple-stall. The old woman observed it and exclaimed:

"Ay, ay, such a sight makes one forgive a great deal"; but he turned his back on her in silence, and joined his friend at the appointed spot.

They made their way without difficulty to the seats reserved for the senators' families, and when they had taken their places, the young man replied but briefly to the sympathetic inquiries as to his health which were addressed to him by his acquaintances. His friend Timon gazed anxiously into his handsome but pale, sad face, as Diodoros sat crushed and absorbed in thought. He would have liked to urge him to quit the scene at once, for the seats just opposite were those destined to Caesar and his court-among them, no doubt, Melissa. In the dim light which still prevailed in the vast amphitheatre it was impossible to recognize faces. But there would soon be a blaze of light, and what misery must await the hapless victim of her faithlessness, still so far from perfect health! After the glare of light outside, which was almost blinding, the twilight within was for the moment a relief to Diodoros. His weary limbs were resting, a pleasant smell came up from the perfumed fountains in the arena, and his eyes, which could not here rest on anything to gratify him, were fixed on vacancy.

And yet it was a comfort to him to think that he had broken his pipe. It would have disgraced him to whistle it; and, moreover, the tone would have reached the ear of the noble lady who had accompanied Melissa, and whom he himself had, only yesterday, revered as a second mother.

Loud music now struck up, he heard shouts and cheers, and just above him —for it could only proceed from the uppermost tiers—there was an extraordinary tumult. Still he paid no heed, and as he thought of that matron the question suddenly arose in his mind, whether she would have consented to be seen with Melissa if she thought that the girl was indeed capable of ruthless falsehood or any other unworthy act. He, who never missed a show in the arena, had never seen the lady Euryale here. She could hardly have come to-day for her own pleasure; she had come, then, for Melissa's sake; and yet she knew that the girl was betrothed to him. Unless Caesar had commanded the matron's presence, Melissa must still be worthy of the esteem and affection of this best of women; and at this reflection Hope once more raised her head in his tortured soul.

He now suddenly wished that brighter light might dispel the gloom which just now he had found so restful; for the lady Euryale's demeanor would show him whether Melissa were still a virtuous maiden. If the matron were as friendly with her as ever, her heart was perhaps still his; it was not the splendor of the purple that had led her astray, but the coercion of the tyrant.

His silent reflections were here interrupted by the loud sounding of trumpets, battle-cries, and, immediately after, the fall of some heavy body, followed by repeated acclamations, noisy outcries, and the applause of those about him. Not till then had he been aware that the performances had begun. Below him, indeed, on the arena from which he had not once raised his eyes, nothing was to be seen on the yellow sand but the scented fountain and a shapeless body, by which a second and a third were soon lying; but overhead something was astir, and, from the right-hand side, bright rays flashed across the wide space. Above the vast circle of seats, arranged on seven tiers, suns and huge, strangely shaped stars were seen, which shed a subdued, many-tinted radiance; and what the youth saw over his head was not the vault of heaven, which to- night bent over his native city darkened by clouds, but a velarium of immense size on which the nocturnal firmament was depicted. This covered in the whole of the open space. Every constellation which rose over Alexandria was plainly recognizable. Jupiter and Mars, Caesar's favorites, outdid the other planets in size and brightness; and in the center of this picture of the sky, which slowly revolved round it, stars were set to form the letters of Caracalla's names, Bassianus and Antoninus. But their light, too, was dim, and veiled as it were with clouds. Soft music was heard from these artificial heavens, and in the stratum of air immediately beneath, the blare of war-trumpets and battle- cries were heard. Thus all eyes were directed upward, and Diodoros's with the rest.

He perceived, with amazement, that the givers of the entertainment, in their anxiety to set something absolutely new before their imperial guest, had arranged that the first games should take place in the air. A battle was being fought overhead, on a level with the highest places, in a way that must surely be a surprise even to the pampered Romans. Black and gold barks were jostling each other in mid-air, and their crews were fighting with the energy of despair. The Egyptian myth of the gods of the great lights who sail the celestial ocean in golden barks, and of the sun-god who each morning conquers the demons of darkness, had suggested the subject of this performance.

The battle between the Spirits of Darkness and of Light was to be fought out high above the best rows of seats occupied by Caesar and his court; and the combatants were living men, for the most part such as had been condemned to death or to the hardest forced labor. The black vessels were manned by negroes, the golden by fair-haired criminals, and they had embarked readily enough; for some of them would escape from the fray with only a few wounds and some quite unhurt, and each one was resolved to use his weapons so as to bring the frightful combat to a speedy end.

The woolly-haired blacks did not indeed know that they had been provided with loosely made swords which would go to pieces at the first shock, and with shields which could not resist a serious blow; while the fair- haired representatives of the light were supplied with sharp and strong weapons of offense and defense. At any cost the spirits of darkness must not be allowed to triumph over those of light. Of what value was a negro's life, especially when it was already forfeited?

While Euryale and Melissa sat with eyes averted from the horrible scene going on above them, and the matron, holding her young companion's hand, whispered to her:

"O child, child! to think that I should be compelled to bring you here!" loud applause and uproarious clapping surrounded them on every side.

The gem-cutter Heron, occupying one of the foremost cushioned seats, radiant with pride and delight in the red-bordered toga of his new dignity, clapped his big hands with such vehemence that his immediate neighbors were almost deafened. He, too, had been badly received, on his arrival, with shrill whistling, but he had been far from troubling himself about that. But when a troop of "Greens" had met him, just in front of the imperial dais, shouting brutal abuse in his face, he had paused, chucked the nearest man under the chin with his powerful fist, and fired a storm of violent epithets at the rest. Thanks to the lictors, he had got off without any harm, and as soon as he found himself among friends and men of rank, on whom he looked in speechless respect, he had recovered his spirits. He was looking forward with intense satisfaction to the moment when he might ask Caesar what he now thought of Alexandria.

Like his father, Alexander was intent on the bloody struggle—gazing upward with breathless interest as the combatants tried to fling each other into the yawning depth below them. But at the same time he never for an instant forgot the insults he had endured outside. How deeply he felt them was legible in his clouded face. Only once did a smile pass over it—when, toward the end of this first fight, the place was made lighter, he perceived in the row of seats next above him the daughter of his neighbor Skopas, pretty Ino, whom but a few days since he had vowed to love. He was conscious of having treated her badly, and given her the right to call him faithless. Toward her, indeed, he had been guilty of treachery, and it had really weighed on his soul. Their eyes met, and she gave him to understand in the plainest way that she had heard him stigmatized as Caesar's spy, and had believed the calumny. The mere sight of him seemed to fill her with anger, and she did her utmost to show him that she had quickly found a substitute for him; and it was to Alexander, no doubt, that Ktesias, her young kinsman, who had long paid her his addresses, owed the kindliness with which Ino now gazed into his eyes. This was some comfort to the luckless, banished lover. On her account, at any rate, he need reproach himself no longer. Diodoros was sitting opposite to him, and his attention, too, was frequently interrupted.

The flashing swords and torches in the hands of the Spirits of Light, and the dimly gleaming stars above their heads, had not so far dispelled the darkness as that the two young people could identify each other. Diodoros, indeed, even throughout this absorbing fight, had frequently glanced at the imperial seats, but had failed to distinguish his beloved from the other women in Caracalla's immediate vicinity. But it now grew lighter, for, while the battle was as yet undecided, a fresh bark, full of Spirits of Light, flourishing their torches, was unexpectedly launched to support their comrades, and Heaven seemed to have sent them forth to win the fight, which had already lasted longer than the masters of the ceremonies had thought possible.

The wild shouts of the combatants and the yells of the wounded had long since drowned the soft music of the spheres above their heads. The call of tubas and bugles rang without ceasing through the great building, to the frequent accompaniment of the most horrible sound of all in this hideous spectacle—the heavy fall of a dead man dropping from above into the gulf.

But this dreadful thud was what gave rise to the loudest applause among the spectators, falling on their satiated ears as a new sound. This frenzied fight in the air, such as had never before been seen, gave rise to the wildest delight, for it led the eye, which was wont in this place to gaze downward, in a direction in which it had never yet been attracted. And what a glorious spectacle it was when black and white wrestled together! How well the contrast of color distinguished the individual combatants, even when they clung together in close embrace! And when, toward the end of the struggle, a bark was overturned bodily, and some of the antagonists would not be parted, even as they fell, trying to kill each other in their rage and hatred, the very walls of the great structure shook with the wild clamor and applause of thousands of every degree.

Only once did the roar of approval reach a higher pitch, and that was after the battle was ended, at what succeeded. Hardly had the victorious Spirits of Light been seen to stand up in their barks, waving their torches, to receive from fluttering genii wreaths of laurel which they flung down to where Caesar sat, than a perfumed vapor, emanating from the place where the painted sky met the wall of the circular building, hid the whole of the upper part of it from the sight of the spectators. The music stopped, and from above there came a strange and ominous growling, hissing, rustling, and crackling. A dull light, dimmer even than before, filled the place, and anxious suspicions took possession of the ten thousand spectators.

What was happening? Was the velarium on fire; had the machinery for lighting up refused to work; and must they remain in this uncomfortable twilight?

Here and there a shout of indignation was heard, or a shrill whistle from the capricious mob. But the mist had already gradually vanished, and those who gazed upward could see that the velarium with the sun and stars had made way for a black surface. No one knew whether this was the real cloudy sky, or whether another, colorless awning closed them in. But suddenly the woven roof parted; invisible hands drew away the two halves. Quick, soft music began as if at a signal from a magician, and at the same time such a flood of light burst down into the theatre that every one covered his eyes with his hand to avoid being blinded. The full glory of sunshine followed on the footsteps of night, like a triumphant chorus on a dismal mourning chant.

The machinists of Alexandria had done wonders. The Romans, who, even at the night performances of the festival of Flora, had never seen the like, hailed the effect with a storm of applause which showed no signs of ceasing, for, when they had sufficiently admired the source of the light which flooded the theatre, reflected from numberless mirrors, and glanced round the auditorium, they began again to applaud with hands and voices. At a given signal thousands of lights appeared round the tiers of seats, and, if the splendor of the entertainment answered at all to that of the Alexandrian spectators, something fine indeed was to be expected.

It was now possible to see the beauty of the women and the costliness of their attire; not till now had the precious stones shown their flashing and changeful radiance. How many gardens and lotus-pools must have been plundered, how many laurel-groves stripped to supply the wreaths which graced every head in the upper rows! And to look round those ranks and note the handsome raiment in which men and women alike were arrayed, suggested a belief that all the inhabitants of Alexandria must be rich. Wherever the eye turned, something beautiful or magnificent was to be seen; and the numerous delightful pictures which crowded on the sight were framed with massive garlands of lotos and mallow, lilies and roses, olive and laurel, tall papyrus and waving palm, branches of pine and willow-here hanging m thick festoons, there twining round the columns or wreathing the pilasters and backs of seats.

Of all the couples in this incomparable amphitheatre one alone neither saw nor heard all that was going on. Scarcely had the darkness given way to light, when Melissa's eyes met those of her lover, and recognition was immediately followed by a swift inquiry and reply which filled the unhappy pair with revived hopes. Melissa's eyes told Diodoros that she loved him and him alone, and she read in his that he could never give her up. Still, his also expressed the doubt and anxiety of his tortured soul, and sent question after question across to Melissa.

And she understood the mute appeal as well as though looks were words. Without heeding the curious crowd about her, or considering the danger of such audacity, she took up her nosegay and waved it toward him as though to refresh him with its fragrance, and then pressed a hasty kiss on the finest of the half-opened buds. His responsive gesture showed that she had been understood, for her lover's expressive eyes beamed with unqualified love and gratitude. Never, she thought, had he gazed more fervently in her face, and again she bent over the bunch of roses.

But even in the midst of her newly found happiness her cheeks tingled with maidenly modesty at her own boldness. Too happy to regret what she had done, but still anxious lest the friend whose opinion was all in all to her should disapprove, she forgot time and place, and, laying her head on Euryale's shoulder, looked up at her in inquiry with her large eyes as though imploring forgiveness. The matron understood, for she had followed the girl's glance and felt what it was that stirred her heart; and, little thinking of the joy she was giving to a third person, she clasped her closely and kissed her on the temple, regardless of the people about them.

At this Diodoros felt as though he had won the prize in a race; and his friend Timon, whose artistic eye was feasting on the magnificent scene, started at the vehement and ardent pressure which Diodoros bestowed on his hand.

What had come over the poor, suffering youth whom he, Timon, had escorted to the Circus out of sheer compassion? His eyes sparkled, and he held his head as high as ever. What was the meaning of his declaring that everything would go well with him now? But it was in vain that he questioned the youth, for Diodoros could not reveal, even to his best friend, what it was that made him happy. It was enough for him to know that Melissa loved him, and that the woman to whom he looked up with enthusiastic reverence esteemed her as highly as ever. And now, for the first time, he began to feel ashamed of his doubts of Melissa. How could he, who had known her from childhood, have believed of her anything so base and foul? It must be some strong compulsion which bound her to Caesar, and she could never have looked at him thus unless she had some scheme—in which, perhaps, the lady Euryale meant to abet her—for escaping her imperial suitor before it was too late. Yes, it must be so; and the oftener he gazed at her the more convinced he felt.

Now he rejoiced in the blaze of light about him, for it showed him his beloved. The words which Euryale had whispered in her ear must have been an admonition to prudence, for she only rarely bestowed on him a loving glance, and he acknowledged that the mute but eager exchange of signals would have been fraught with danger for both of them.

The first sudden illumination had revealed too many things to distract the attention of the spectators, including Caesar's, for their proceedings to be observed. Now curiosity was to some extent satisfied, and even Diodoros felt that reserve was imperative.

Caracalla had not yet shown himself to the people. A golden screen, in which there were holes for him to look through without being seen, hid him from public gaze; still Diodoros could recognize those who were admitted to his presence. First came the givers of the entertainment; then the Parthian envoys, and some delegates from the municipal authorities of the town. Finally, Seleukus presented the wives of the magnates who had shared with him the cost of this display, and among these, all magnificently dressed, the lady Berenike shone supreme by the pride of her demeanor and the startling magnificence of her attire. As her large eyes met those of Caesar with a flash of defiance, he frowned, and remarked satirically:

"It seems to be the custom here to mourn in much splendor!"

But Berenike promptly replied:

"It has nothing to do with mourning. It is in honor of the sovereign who commanded the presence of the mourner at the Circus."

Diodoros could not see the flame of rage in, Caesar's threatening eye, nor hear his reply to the audacious matron:

"This is a misapprehension of how to do me honor, but an opportunity will occur for teaching the Alexandrians better."

Even across the amphitheatre the youth could see the sudden flush and pallor of the lady's haughty face; and immediately after, Macrinus, the praetorian prefect, approached Caracalla with the master of the games, the superintendent of the school of gladiators.

At the same time Diodoros heard his next neighbor, a member of the city senate, say:

"How quietly it is going off! My proposal that Caesar should come in to a dim light, so as to keep him and his unpopular favorites out of sight for a while, has worked capitally. Who could the mob whistle at, so long as they could not see one from another? Now they are too much delighted to be uproarious. Caesar's bride, of all others, has reason to thank me. And she reminds me of the Persian warriors who, before going into battle, bound cats to their bucklers because they knew that the Egyptian foe would not shoot at them so long as the sacred beasts were exposed to being hit by his arrows."

"What do you mean by that?" asked another, and received the brisk reply:

"The lady Euryale is the cat who protects the damsel. Out of respect for her, and for fear of hurting her, too, her companion has hitherto been spared even by those fellows up there."

And he pointed to a party of "Greens" who were laying their heads together in one of the topmost tiers. But his friend replied:

"Something besides that keeps them within bounds. The three beardless fellows just behind them belong to the city watch, who are scattered through the general mass like raisins in doughcakes."

"That is very judicious," replied the senator.

"We might otherwise have had to quit the Circus a great deal quicker than we came in. We shall hardly get home with dry garments as it is. Look how the lights up there are flaring; you can hear the lashing of the storm, and such flashes are not produced by machinery. Zeus is preparing his bolts, and if the storm bursts—"

Here his discourse was interrupted by the sound of trumpets, mingling with the roar of distant thunder following a vivid flash. The procession now began, which was the preliminary to every such performance.

The statues of the gods had, before Caesar's arrival, been placed on the pedestals erected for them to prevent any risk of a demonstration at the appearance of the deified emperors. The priests now first marched solemnly round these statues, and Timotheus poured a libation on the sand to Serapis, while the priest of Alexandria did the same to the tutelary hero of the town. Then the masters of the games, the gladiators, and beast-fighters came out, who were to make proof of their skill. As the priests approached Caesar's dais, Caracalla came forward and greeted the spectators, thus showing himself for the first time.

While he was still sitting behind the screen, he had sent for Melissa, who had obeyed the command, under the protection of Euryale, and he had spoken to her graciously. He now took no further notice of her, of her father, or her brother, and by his orders their places had been separated by some little distance from his. By the advice of Timotheus he would not let her be seen at his side till the stars had once more been consulted, and he would then conduct Melissa to the Circus as his wife- the day after to-morrow, perhaps. He thanked the matron for having escorted Melissa, and added, with a braggart air of virtue, that the world should see that he, too, could sacrifice the most ardent wish of his heart to moral propriety.

The elephant torch-bearers had greatly delighted him, and in the expectation of seeing Melissa again, and of a public recognition that he had won the fairest maid there, he had come into the Circus in the best spirits. He still wore his natural expression; yet now and then his brow was knit, for he was haunted by the eyes of Seleukus's wife. The haughty woman—"that bedizened Niobe" he had contemptuously called her in speaking to Macrinus—had appeared to him as an avenging goddess; strangely enough, every time he thought of her, he remembered, too, the consul Vindex and his nephew, whose execution Melissa's intercession had only hastened, and he was vexed now that he had not lent an ear to her entreaties. The fact that the name Vindex signified an avenger disturbed him greatly, and he could no more get it out of his mind than the image of the "Niobe" with her ominous dark eyes.

He would see her no more; and in this he was helped by the gladiators, for they now approached him, and their frantic enthusiasm kept him for some time from all other thoughts. While they flourished their weapons- some the sword and buckler, and others the not less terrible net and harpoon—the time-honored cry rose from their husky throats in eager acclamation: "Hail, Caesar! those about to die salute thee!" Then, in rows of ten men each, they crossed the arena at a rapid pace.

Between the first and second group one man swaggered past alone, as though he were something apart, and he strutted and rolled as he walked with pompous self-importance. It was his prescriptive right, and in his broad, coarse features, with a snub nose, thick lips, and white, flashing teeth like those of a beast of prey, it was easy to see that the adversary would fare but ill who should try to humble him. And yet he was not tall; but on his deep chest, his enormous square shoulders, and short, bandy legs, the muscles stood out like elastic balls, showing the connoisseur that in strength he was a giant. A loin-cloth was all he wore, for he was proud of the many scars which gleamed red and white on his fair skin. He had pushed back his little bronze helmet, so that the terrible aspect of the left side of his face might not be lost on the populace. While he was engaged in fighting three panthers and a lion, the lion had torn out his eye and with it part of his cheek. His name was Tarautas, and he was known throughout the empire as the most brutal of gladiators, for he had also earned the further privilege of never fighting but for life or death, and never under any circumstances either granting or asking quarter. Where he was engaged corpses strewed the plain.

Caesar knew that he himself had been nicknamed Tarautas after this man, and he was not ill pleased; for, above all things, he aimed at being thought strong and terrible, and this the gladiator was without a peer in his own rank of life. They knew each other: Tarautas had received many a gift from his imperial patron after hard-won victories in which his blood had flowed. And now, as the scarred veteran, who, puffed up with conceit, walked singly and apart in the long train of gladiators, cast a roving and haughty glance on the ranks of spectators, he was filled out of due time with the longing to center all eyes on himself, the one aim of his so frequently risking his life in these games. His chest swelled, he braced up the tension of his supple sinews, and as he passed the imperial seats he whirled his short sword round his head, describing a circle in the air, with such skill and such persistent rapidity, that it appeared like a disk of flashing steel. At the same time his harsh, powerful voice bellowed out, "Hail, Caesar!" sounding above the shouts of his comrades like the roar of a lion; and Caracalla, who had not yet vouchsafed a friendly word or pleasant look to any Alexandrian, waved his hand graciously again and again to this audacious monster, whose strength and skill delighted him.

This was the instant for which the "Greens" in the third tier were waiting. No one could prohibit their applauding the man whom Caesar himself approved, so they forthwith began shouting "Tarautas!" with all their might. They knew that this would suggest the comparison between Caesar and the sanguinary wretch whose name had been applied to him, and all who were eager to give expression to their vexation or dissatisfaction took the hint and joined in the outcry. Thus in a moment the whole amphitheatre was ringing with the name of "Tarautas!"

At first it rose here and there; but soon, no one knew how, the whole crowd in the upper ranks joined in one huge chorus, giving free vent to their long-suppressed irritation with childish and increasing uproar, shouting the word with steady reiteration and a sort of involuntary rhythm. Before long it sounded as though the multitude must have practiced the mad chant which swelled to a perfect roar.

"Tarau-Tarau-Tarautas!" and, as is always the case when a breach has been made in the dam, one after another joined in, with here the shrill whistle of a reed pipe and there the clatter of a rattle. Mingling with these were the angry outcries of those whom the lictors or guardians of the peace had laid hands on, or their indignant companions; and the thunder outside rolled a solemn accompaniment to the mutinous tumult within.

Caesar's scowling brow showed that a storm threatened in that quarter also; and no sooner had he discerned the aim of the crowd than, foaming with rage, he commanded Macrinus to restore order.

Then, above the chaos of voices, trumpet-calls were sounded. The masters of the games perceived that, if only they could succeed in riveting the attention of the mob by some exciting or interesting scene, that would surely silence the demonstration which was threatening ruin to the whole community; so the order was at once given to begin the performance with the most important and effective scene with which it had been intended that the whole should conclude.

The spectacle was to represent a camp of the Alemanni, surprised and seized by Roman warriors. In this there was a covert compliment to Caesar, who, after a doubtful victory over that valiant people, had assumed the name of Alemannicus. Part of the gladiators, clothed in skins, represented the barbarians, and wore long flowing wigs of red or yellow hair; others played the part of Roman troops, who were to conquer them. The Alemanni were all condemned criminals, who were allowed no armor, and only blunt swords wherewith to defend themselves. But life and freedom were promised to the women if, after the camp was seized, they wounded themselves with the sharp knives with which each one was provided, at least deeply enough to draw blood. And any who succeeded in feigning death really deceptively were to earn a special reward. Among the Germans there were, too, a few gladiators of exceptional stature, armed with sharp weapons, so as to defer the decision for a while.

In a few minutes, and under the eyes of the spectators, carts, cattle, and horses were placed together in a camp, and surrounded by a wall of tree trunks, stones, and shields. Meanwhile shouts and whistles were still heard; nay, when Tarautas came out on the arena in the highly decorated armor of a Roman legate, at the head of a troop of heavily armed men, and again greeted the emperor, the commotion began afresh. But Caracalla's patience was exhausted, and the high-priest saw by his pale cheeks and twitching eyelids what was passing in his mind; so, inspired by the fervent hope of averting some incalculable disaster from his fellow-citizens, he took his place in front of the statue of the god, and, lifting up his hands, he began:

"In the name of Serapis, O Macedonians!" His deep, ringing tones sounded above the voices of the insurgents in the upper rows, and there was silence.

Not a sound was to be heard but the long-drawn howling of the wind, and now and then the flap of a strip of cloth torn from the velarium by the gale. Mingling with these might be heard the uncanny hooting of owls and daws which the illumination had brought out of their nests in the cornice, and which the storm was now driving in again.

Timotheus, in a clear and audible address, now appealed to his audience to remain quiet, not to disturb the splendid entertainment here set before them, and above all to remember that great Caesar, the divine ruler of the world, was in their midst, an honor to each and all. As the guest of the most hospitable city on earth, their illustrious sovereign had a right to expect from every Alexandrian the most ardent endeavors to make his stay here delightful. It was his part as high-priest to uplift his warning voice in the name of the greatest of the gods, that the ill- will of a few malcontents might not give rise to an idea in the mind of their beloved guest that the natives of Alexandria were blind to the blessings for which every citizen had to thank his beneficent rule.

A shrill whistle here interrupted his discourse, and a voice shouted: "What blessings? We know of none."

But Timotheus was not to be checked, and went on more vehemently

"All of you who, by the grace of Caesar, have been made Roman citizens—"

But again a voice broke in—the speaker was the overseer of the granaries of Seleukus, sitting in the second tier—"And do you suppose we do not know what the honor costs us?"

This query was heartily applauded, and then suddenly, as if by magic, a perfect chorus arose, chanting a distich which one man in the crowd had first given out and then two or three had repeated, to which a fourth had given a sort of tune, till it was shouted by every one present at the very top of his voice, with marked application to him of whom it spoke. From the topmost row of places, on every side of the amphitheatre, rang out the following lines, which but a moment before no one had ever heard:

"Death to the living, to pay for burying those that are dead; Since, what the taxes have spared, soldiers have ruthlessly seized."

And the words certainly came from the heart; of the people, for they seemed never weary of repeating them; and it was not till a tremendous clap of thunder shook the very walls that several were silent and looked up with increasing alarm. The moment's pause was seized on to begin the fight.

Caesar bit his lip in powerless fury, and his hatred of the towns-people, who had thus so plainly given him to understand their sentiments, was rising from one minute to the next. He felt it a real misfortune that he was unable to punish on the spot the insult thus offered him; swelling with rage, he remembered a speech made by Caligula, and wished the town had but one head, that he might sever it from the body. The blood throbbed so fiercely in his temples, and there was such a singing in his ears, that for some little time he neither saw nor heard what was going on. This terrible agitation might cost him yet some hours of great suffering. But he need no longer dread them so much; for there sat the living remedy which he believed he had secured by the strongest possible ties.

How fair she was! And, as he looked round once more at Melissa, he observed that her eye was turned on him with evident anxiety. At this a light seemed to dawn in his clouded soul, and he was once more conscious of the love which had blossomed in his heart. But it would never do to make her who had wrought the miracle so soon the confidante of his hatred. He had seen her angry, had seen her weep, and had seen her smile; and within the next few days, which were to make him a happy man instead of a tortured victim, he longed only to see her great eyes sparkle and her lips overflow with words of love, joy, and gratitude. His score with the Alexandrians must be settled later, and it was in his power to make them atone with their blood and bitterly rue the deeds of this night.

He passed his hand over his furrowed brow, as though to wake himself from a bad dream; nay, he even found a smile when next his eyes met hers; and those spectators to whom his aspect seemed more absorbing than the horrible slaughter in the arena, looked at each other in amazement, for the indifference or the dissimulation, whichever it might be, with which Caesar regarded this unequaled scene of bloodshed, seemed to them quite incredible.

Never, since his very first visit to a circus, had Caracalla left unnoticed for so long a time the progress of such a battle as this. However, nothing very remarkable had so far occurred, for the actual seizure of the camp had but just begun with the massacre of the Alemanni and the suicide of the women.

At this moment the gladiator Tarautas, as nimble as a cat and as bloodthirsty as a hungry wolf, sprang on to one of the enemy's piled-up wagons, and a tall swordsman, with a bear-skin over his shoulder, and long, reddish-gold hair, flew to meet him.

This was no sham German! Caracalla knew the man. He had been brought to Rome among the captive chiefs, and, as he had proved to be a splendid horseman, he had found employment in Caesar's stables. His conduct had always been blameless till, on the day when Caracalla had entered Alexandria, he had, in a drunken fit, killed first the man set over him, a hot-headed Gaul, and then the two lictors who had attempted to apprehend him. He was condemned to death, and had been placed on the German side to fight for his life in the arena.

And how he fought! How he defied the most determined of gladiators, and parried his strokes with his short sword! This was a combat really worth watching; indeed, it so captivated Caracalla that he forgot everything else. The name of the German's antagonist had been applied to him— Caesar. Just now the many-voiced yell "Tarautas!" had been meant for him; and, accustomed as he was to read an omen in every incident, he said to himself, and called Fate to witness, that the gladiator's doom would foreshadow his own. If Tarautas fell, then Caesar's days were numbered; if he triumphed, then a long and happy life would be his.

He could leave the decision to Tarautas with perfect confidence; he was the strongest gladiator in the empire, and he was fighting with a sharp sword against the blunt one in his antagonist's hand, who probably had forgotten in the stable how to wield the sword as he had done of yore. But the German was the son of a chief, and had followed arms from his earliest youth. Here it was defense for dear life, however glorious it might be to die under the eyes of the man whom he had learned to honor as the conqueror and tyrant of many nations, among them his own. So the strong and practiced athlete did his best.

He, like his opponent, felt that the eyes of ten thousand were on him, and he also longed to purge himself of the dishonor which, by actual murder, he had brought on himself and on the race of which he was still a son. Every muscle of his powerful frame gained more rigid tension at the thought, and when he was presently hit by the sword of his hitherto unconquered foe, and felt the warm blood flow over his breast and left arm, he collected all his strength. With the battle-cry of his tribe, he flung his huge body on the gladiator. Heedless of the furious sword- thrust with which Tarautas returned the assault, he threw himself off the top of the packed wagon on to the stones of the camp inclosure, and the combatants rolled, locked together like one man, from the wall into the sand of the arena.

Caracalla started as though he himself had been the injured victim, and watched, but in vain, to see the supple Tarautas, who had escaped such perils before now, free himself from the weight of the German's body.

But the struggle continued to rage round the pair, and neither stirred a finger. At this Caesar, greatly disturbed, started to his feet, and desired Theocritus to make inquiry as to whether Tarautas were wounded or dead; and while the favorite was gone he could not sit still. Agitated by distressing fears, he rose to speak first to one and then to another of his suite, only to drop on his seat again and glance once more at the butchery below. He was fully persuaded that his own end must be near, if indeed Tarautas were dead. At last he heard Theocritus's voice, and, as he turned to ask him the news, he met a look from the lady Berenike, who had risen to quit the theatre.

He shuddered!—the image of Vindex and his nephew rose once more before his mind's eye; at the same moment, however, Theocritus hailed him with the exclamation:

"That fellow, Tarautas, is not a man at all! I should call him an eel if he were not so broad shouldered. The rascal is alive, and the physician says that in three weeks he will be ready again to fight four bears or two Alemanni!"

A light as of sudden sunshine broke on Caesar's face, and he was perfectly cheerful again, though a fearful clap of thunder rattled through the building, and one of those deluges of rain which are known only in the south came pouring down into the open theatre, extinguishing the fires and lights, and tearing the velarium from its fastenings till it hung flapping in the wind and lashing the upper tiers of places, so as to drive the spectators to a hasty retreat.

Men were flying, women screaming and sobbing, and the heralds loudly proclaimed that the performance was suspended, and would be resumed on the next day but one.

Milton Keynes UK
Ingram Content Group UK Ltd.
UKHW011105080324
439029UK00005B/457